The TINDIMS and the TEN GREEN BOTTLES

Mother-daughter duo,
Sally Gardner and Lydia Corry
are keen conservationists. Sally
is a Costa and Carnegie-winning
author and Lydia's *Eight Princesses
and a Magic Mirror*, was a
Guardian Book of the Year 2019.
Ten Green Bottles is the third
book in this series following
The Tindims of Rubbish Island and
The Tindims and the Turtle Tangle.

Also by

Sally Gardner & Lydia Corry

The Tindims of Rubbish Island
The Tindims and the Turtle Tangle

The TINDIMS

and the Ten Green Bottles

Sally Gardner & Lydia Corry

ZEPHYR

an imprint of Head of Zeus

First published in the UK by Zephyr,
an imprint of Head of Zeus, in 2021

9 7 5 3 1 2 4 6 8

A catalogue record for this book is available
from the British Library.

ISBN (PB): 9781838935719
ISBN (E): 9781838935726

Typesetting & design by Jessie Price

Printed and bound in Great Britain
by CPI Group (UK) Ltd, Croydon CR0 4YY

Head of Zeus Ltd
First Floor East
5–8 Hardwick Street
London EC1R 4RG

www.headofzeus.com

To Adrian,
a very special
Long Leg.

From SG and LC

hello!

Chapter One

Where Granny Gull and Barnacle Bow find out they need ten green bottles to welcome a special visitor to Rubbish Island.

ranny Gull and
Barnacle Bow had,
that neeptide, been
busily hanging wallpaper in
their houseboat. Granny Gull
had made it from dried-out
pieces of wrapping paper that
she and Barnacle Bow had scooped
from the briny sea.

It was while Barnacle Bow was
up a ladder, with brush and bucket,
that a thought came to Granny Gull.
She wondered if there were still
ten green glass bottles on
Rubbish Island. They had
hundreds, if not thousands,
of plastic bottles. But
they were no use for a
Bottlerama.

A BOTTLERAMA is a traditional
musical instrument played to welcome
a visitor to the island. It is made from
ten green glass bottles and the music it
makes sounds as if the clouds are singing.
But as Rubbish Island hadn't had a visitor
for ages, or maybe even longer, there
hadn't been a need for one.

'Do you think,' said Granny Gull to
Barnacle Bow, 'that we still have ten
green glass bottles?'

4

Barnacle Bow said, 'That is an excellent question. I don't know.'

Granny Gull was looking through the window, out to the sea. She polished her glasses and looked again. 'Because I think,' she said, 'we are going to need a Bottlerama today.'

Barnacle Bow laughed. 'But we have had no visitors for years and years.'

Granny Gull said, 'Do you see what I see?'

Barnacle Bow scratched his head. 'Yes, the new wallpaper looks grand.'

'No,' said Granny Gull, and she pointed out of the window.

In the distance was a ship. There was no mistaking who it belonged to.

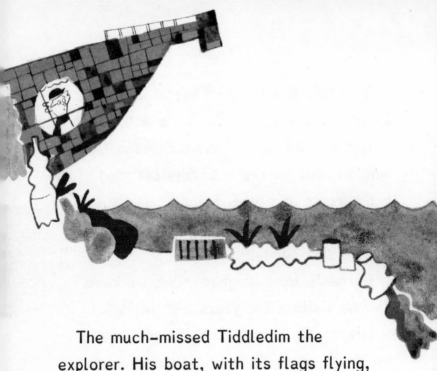

The much-missed Tiddledim the
explorer. His boat, with its flags flying,
was making its way towards Turtle Bay.

'Musical mussels! I don't believe
it,' said Barnacle Bow. 'Now we most
definitely need to find ten green bottles.
Do you think we might have a glass
bottle in the houseboat?'

They looked high and low. Not a
glass bottle could they find. Barnacle
Bow said he would ask Ethel B Dina.

After all, she was the last Tindim to play the Bottlerama.

Granny Gull said, 'We still have some time before Tiddledim is here. He has to weigh anchor before he comes ashore. I'm going to bake cakes and muflops,' which is a Tindim way of saying muffins. 'There's nothing better to welcome a Tindim home than a proper sit-down tea, one with a tablecloth and napkins.'

Chapter Two

Where the search is on to find ten green bottles in time for Tiddledim's arrival.

*B*arnacle Bow set off towards the fish hospital.

'Hello, my still and sparkling darling,' said Ethel when she saw him. 'We are back in cold water, so the walrus tells me.'

Barnacle Bow wasn't listening. All he could think about was ten green bottles. 'Do you happen to know where the Bottlerama is?' he asked.

'Why?' said Ethel B Dina. 'We only need to play it if there's a visitor and we don't have a—'

'Tiddledim the explorer is coming into Turtle Bay,' interrupted Barnacle Bow. 'Granny Gull is baking cakes and we need the Bottlerama.'

'It
was put
away ages
ago,' said
Ethel. 'I've
forgotten
where.'

First they
searched the fish hospital. Then they
searched the Garden of Wonders, where
they found one green bottle which was
part of a water fountain.

'I do hope we don't have to use that
one,' said Ethel B Dina. 'It looks so
pretty in the fountain.'

Finally, in a cupboard in the library,
they found the Bottlerama. It was a sad
sight, with only two bottles left.

'I think,' said Barnacle Bow, 'things
looked better before we found it.'

'How's that?' asked Ethel B Dina.

'Because before we found it, there was still hope it might have a full set of ten green bottles, instead of just two.' He sighed. 'And even if we had ten green bottles, they would be no good with this broken old instrument.'

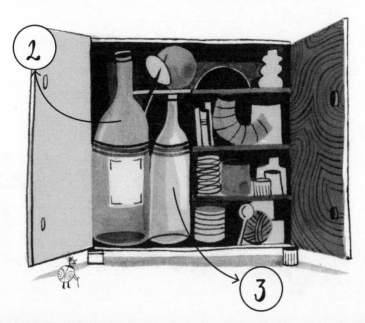

'You're right,' said Ethel B Dina. 'But if we could find ten green bottles, Spokes could make a new one.'

'Not in time for Tiddledim's arrival.'

'We mustn't give up,' said Ethel B Dina. 'It might still be possible. Spokes is a wonder. Where there's a will, Tindims always find a way. We have three bottles so far, if we count the bottle from the water fountain.'

'It's not enough,' said Barnacle Bow.

'Let's go and ask Hitch Stitch,' they said together.

They made their way to Hitch Stitch's house. Hitch Stitch was fond of glass bottles, especially those with messages

inside them. Unfortunately, she only had one left, a pretty little green bottle that was old and magical.

'It will sound lovely in a Bottlerama,' she said.

'Four is not enough,' said Barnacle Bow again. 'We need to find another six bottles and time is not on our side.'

Hitch Stitch thought for a moment, then said, 'Maybe Jug and Mug have one.'

'Or Captain Spoons and Admiral Bonnet. Or Spokes,' said Ethel B Dina.

'There's Broom as well,' said Barnacle Bow.

So, off they went, as fast as Tindim
legs would let them. They were on their
way to see Broom, the gardener, when
they saw Pinch, Skittle's furry purry pet.
He was with the purrtle, who he'd looked
after since it was a chick. Now it was
nearly a fully grown bird. And small it
wasn't.

'Oh, my still and sparkling darling,'
said Ethel B Dina, 'we are in search of
six green glass bottles. Have you seen
one, perhaps two, even three or four?
Five would be fabulous, and six, well, six
bottles would be just what we need.'

Pinch shook his head. 'But I could ask Skittle and Brew,' he said. 'Why do you need them?'

Ethel B Dina told him.

'You mean,' said Pinch, 'that Tiddledim the explorer's ship is coming into Turtle Bay? The same Tiddledim who wrote the book?'

'Yes,' said Hitch Stitch. 'That is why we need ten green bottles. I must hurry.'

'Wait a minute,' said Pinch. 'I have seen one, in the treehouse.'

'Then bring it down to Turtle Bay,' shouted Ethel B Dina. 'And don't dilly-dally. If you see Skittle and Brew, tell them to go to Mug and Jug's house. Perhaps they have one.'

'Will do,' said Pinch, who thought that this was the most exciting thing to have happened since his own turtle tangle adventure. Off he went, bounding along the path towards the treehouse, with the purrtle hurtling behind him.

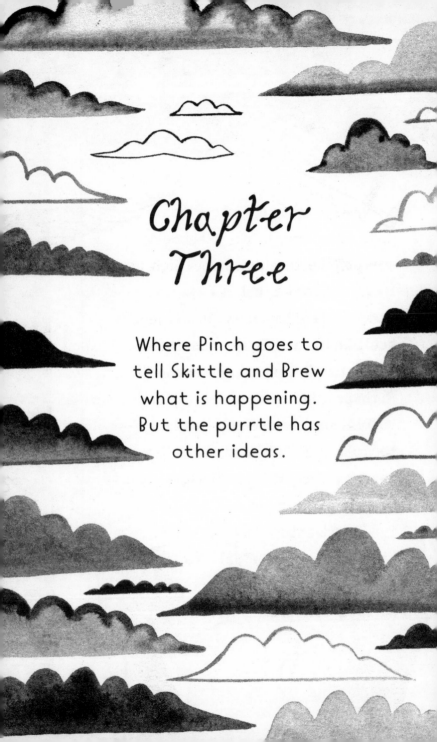

Chapter Three

Where Pinch goes to
tell Skittle and Brew
what is happening.
But the purrtle has
other ideas.

A slipper-slider saw

A tiggletoggle driver

he treehouse was high up in the Roo-Roo trees. It was most probably the best treehouse ever, in the whole vast sea of everything. That's what Skittle and Brew thought.

Spokes had built it out of driftwood. It had taken him quite a long time to collect so much wood. Wood, unlike plastic bottles, doesn't bob up every day.

An upperlooper holder

19

To reach the treehouse they had to
climb a rope ladder which Hitch Stitch,
the queen of knots, had made. There
was a bucket lift for Pinch, so he could
go up and down.

Because, as Pinch said, 'Tails and
paws don't work well with rope ladders,
and that's a fact!'

Pinch tapped the bottle next to the
treehouse and Skittle lowered the bucket.
The purrtle, not wishing to be left behind,
jumped into the bucket as well, so it was
quite a tight squeeze.

'Have you noticed,' said Brew, 'that the purrtle is getting bigger?'

'And heavier,' said Skittle as the bucket slowly made its way up.

Finally they arrived. Skittle and Brew helped Pinch and the purrtle out. Before Pinch could say 'thank you' or 'hello', the purrtle had wandered off. Brew caught hold of it.

'It seems very eager to explore,' said Brew.

'It's never been interested in going off by itself before,' said Pinch.

'Perhaps it's reached the age when it needs to spread its wings,' said Skittle.

'Purrtles don't fly actually,' said Pinch, 'and that's a fact.'

'How do you know it's a fact?' asked Skittle, who was busy sweeping the treehouse. 'Was that in Tiddledim the explorer's book?'

'That's why I'm here,' said Pinch. 'We need to find,' and he counted on his paws, 'six — or was that five? — green glass bottles.'

'Why?' asked Brew.

'Because Tiddledim the explorer's ship is coming into Turtle Bay.'

'Scrunch me a teabag,' said Brew. 'Is that true?'

'Yes,' said Pinch. 'It's the most exciting fact I know.'

They began to look for glass bottles. They looked up in the crow's nest and along the walkways.

'Are you sure,' said Skittle, 'that you have seen a glass bottle here?'

It was then that Pinch remembered. At the bottom of the treehouse, next to the bucket lift, Spokes had hung a glass bottle. Pinch tapped the bottle every time he wanted a lift. He had used it so often that he had forgotten it was there, right under his nose.

'I should have seen it straight away,' said Pinch.

'Often,' said Skittle, 'it's harder to find things that are right under your nose.'

'*That's a fact*,' said Pinch.

They were so thrilled they'd found
another bottle, and were about to climb
down the ladder when Pinch remembered
his purrtle. It was too late.

The purrtle had taken off down the walkway, building speed as it went. As it reached the end, it spread its wings.

'No!' cried Pinch.

There was a whooshing sound, then a flash of orange, red and purple as the spotted wings of a never-seen-before flying purrtle glided over Rubbish Island, into the blue sky and across the grey waves.

'Wow,' said Brew. 'Scrunch me a teabag. I thought you said purrtles can't fly.'

'Maybe,' said Skittle, 'it has gone to welcome Tiddledim.'

Pinch sang sadly:

'Oh, Purrtle, I never knew you could fly
Find your wings and own the sky.
I see now what I always knew
That I am I and you are you.'

'That's the right way to think about it,' said Skittle as they made their way down from the treehouse. Which never seemed as much fun as making their way up.

Hitch Stitch was waiting for them at the bottom, looking up at the glass bottle.

Skittle helped her unhook it.

'Why the sad face?' she said to Pinch.

'Because my purrtle flew away.'

'Oh dear,' said Hitch Stitch, seeing how upset Pinch was. 'Looking after a purrtle is hard work. You gave him the confidence to fly. I would say that is a job well done.'

5

Pinch cheered up a little bit.

'And,' said Hitch Stitch, 'you found a green bottle, which means we only have...'

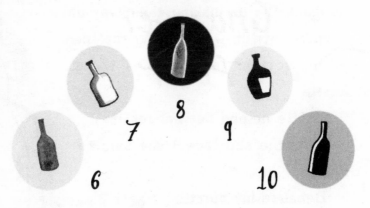

'Five green bottles to find,' said Skittle. 'Ethel and Barnacle Bow have found three. You had one, and we've just found this one. So, we are still five short.'

'Oh dear,' said Hitch Stitch again, 'Tiddledim will soon be here. Go and tell your mum and dad, Brew. And ask if they have any bottles.'

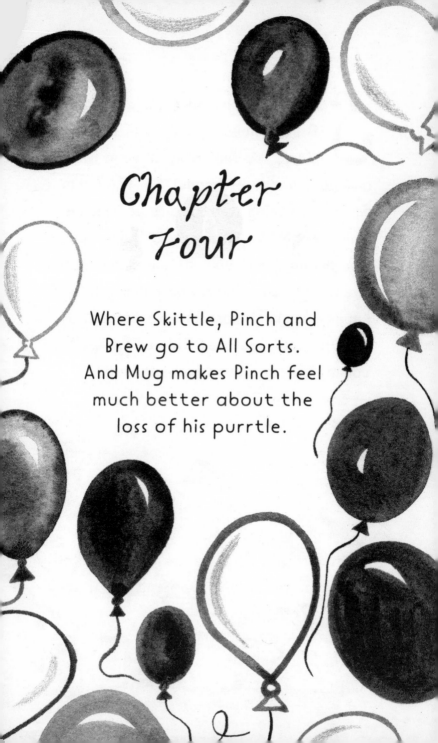

Chapter Four

Where Skittle, Pinch and
Brew go to All Sorts.
And Mug makes Pinch feel
much better about the
loss of his purrtle.

S kittle, Pinch and Brew arrived at Brew's house, which was called All Sorts, to find Brew's mum, Mug, making a badge of honour for Tiddledim. She was making it from bits and pieces in her Might Be Useful box. Baby Cup was helping. She was sitting in her bottle chair, covered in glue and paper and happily sticking more bits to herself.

'Who told you that Tiddledim was coming?' Brew asked his dad, Jug.

'Barnacle Bow,' said Jug. 'He also said the Bottlerama was broken.'

'I thought,' said Mug, 'a badge might be the next best thing. That is, after one of Granny Gull's famous teas.'

Baby Cup called out, 'Glee, glee.'

'She looks like a strange kind of fish,' said Brew.

'It will wash off,' said Mug and they burst out laughing. Pinch felt better for laughing. Then he told Mug about his purrtle.

'Why, that's wonderful,' said Mug.

'But what if it doesn't come back again?' said Pinch.

'It will,' said Mug. 'Now, tell me your poem.'

Pinch did.

'Can we look around, in case you have a green bottle somewhere?' asked Skittle.

'Of course,' said Jug. 'Ten green bottles for the Bottlerama. It's ages since I heard those sweet notes. We've not had a visitor for a long time. How many bottles have you got?'

'Five,' said Brew.

They set about looking, until there was nowhere left to look.

'What we now know,' said Jug, 'is that we don't have any green bottles hidden away anywhere.'

'Does that mean,' said Pinch, 'we won't be able to welcome Tiddledim the explorer home and he will sail away without a hello? If that happens, it will be a terrible day. No purrtle and no Tiddledim.'

'No, Pinch,' said Jug. 'That won't happen. We are so excited he has come home. Think of all the adventures he's had and the many Long Legs he must have seen. I am stuffed full of questions I want to ask him.'

'Me too,' said Brew and Skittle
together.

'And me,' said Mug.

Baby Cup started to giggle and said,
'Silly soggy socks.'

Mug laughed and soon they were all
laughing. Laughter, as any Tindim will tell
you, is the best cure for sadness and for
not finding what you are looking for.

'Perhaps,' said Pinch, 'Tiddledim the explorer will know where my purrtle might be.'

'Now,' said Mug, 'that is a much better way, Pinch, to look at the problem.'

'I think,' said Pinch, 'you are right.'

And with that cheerful thought, Skittle, Pinch and Brew left Mug finishing off the badge. They went to find Skittle's dad, Captain Spoons, singing as they went:

'Purrtle, I never knew you could fly
Find your wings
and own the sky.'

Chapter Five

Where we find Captain
Spoons asleep in a hammock.
And Admiral Bonnet worries
that she might have steered
Rubbish Island into the Land
of the Midnight Sun.

Captain Spoons hadn't looked out to sea that morning. Instead he'd been busy hanging up his new hammock. It had been handwoven by Mug, made out of the many plastic bags she had recycled from the sea.

He lay in the hammock and thought
about plastic bottles and Bottle Hill.
'You get rid of a mountain,' he said
sleepily, 'and a hill starts to grow in its
place.'

Captain Spoons started to count the clouds in the sky. He'd found that counting clouds had much the same effect as counting plastic bottles, both made him fall fast asleep. Soon he was dreaming he'd made a machine which could eat plastic bottles and that Bottle Hill had a hole at its centre which you could see through.

He was so flabbergasted to be woken up that he spun his hammock round and round, until he became tangled up in it.

'You look, Dad,' said Skittle, 'like a roly-poly pastry.'

'Trumpets and tin hats,' said Captain Spoons, untangling himself.

'Tiddledim the explorer's ship is coming into Turtle Bay,' said Broom.

'You mean here, now? The great Tiddledim himself? The one and only? That explorer is coming to Rubbish Island? Well, play the Bottlerama, bring out the spoons and let the party begin.'

He danced a jig on the spot and then stopped all of a sudden. 'Wait, wait, we need cakes, flags, a poem, a song and ten green bottles.'

'We only have five green bottles,' said Brew.

'Five,' said Captain Spoons. 'That will never do. You can't play a Bottlerama without ten green bottles. It's impossible. This is a disaster. What will Tiddledim think of us, with no music to greet him and no song to be sung?'

'The Bottlerama is busted,' said Brew.

'Busted? It can't be,' said Captain Spoons.

'Granny Gull is baking cakes and muflops,' said Skittle. 'She thinks he will be pleased to have his feet on dry land.'

'All we need is for you to come down to the beach with Admiral Bonnet,' said Brew.

Admiral Bonnet was in the kitchen looking at maps and charts.

'There you
are,' said
Captain Spoons.

'Do you know,'
she said, 'I think
we've gone too far
north, and we are
now in the Land of the
Midnight Sun.'

'Never mind that,' said Captain Spoons.
'Tiddledim the explorer has come home.
My dear seaworthy Admiral, we must go
and meet him at once at Turtle Bay.'

Chapter Six

Where Tiddledim
arrives. And there
are more questions
than answers.

*I*t was the jolliest sight to see the
Tindims gathered on the beach. The
tables and chairs had been put out
for tea and the flags were flying. Broom
had brought a large bunch of flowers with
him.

Spokes arrived and said that he had looked, but there were no green glass bottles hidden in the engine room.

'Glass bottles?' asked Broom. 'Why is everyone looking for glass bottles?'

'For the Bottlerama,' said Spokes.

'Oh,' said Broom. 'Of course, the old one we have wouldn't play now, even if you did find ten green bottles. I mean, how long ago is it since it was used?'

'You have a point and it's sharp enough to pop my bubble of worry,' said Captain Spoons.

'It would help,' said Broom,
'if plastic bottles made a
tune. After all, we have more
than enough of them.'

'Look, Dad,' said Skittle.

In the distance, they could see Tiddledim's ship had weighed anchor. Tiddledim had climbed into a rowing boat and started to row towards the beach.

Ethel B Dina was wearing her swan lifesaver ring that she only wore on special occasions. She said, 'As you all know, without a working Bottlerama, I can't sing a welcome home song.'

'Perhaps we could hum,' suggested Admiral Bonnet.

'No,' said Ethel B Dina. 'That would never do.'

Granny Gull put the cakes and muflops on the table and said, 'Now is not the time to worry about it.'

Granny Gull was right. The minute Tiddledim landed, there was so much talking and laughing that a song and the music of a Bottlerama would have had trouble finding space enough to be heard.

It was when they were seated that Ethel B Dina stood up and said, 'It is so good to see you again. I am supposed to sing a song to greet you, accompanied by the gentle chords of a Bottlerama. But we don't have ten green bottles to our name.'

'My dear lady of the still and sparkling delights,' said Tiddledim. 'All I can say is I certainly agree. Without ten green bottles, how can you play the Bottlerama?'

'Glee?' asked Granny Gull.

Skittle, Pinch and Brew couldn't remember anyone else ever having visited Rubbish Island before.

'This is a first,' whispered Skittle to Brew.

Tiddledim sat at the head of the table as Granny Gull poured the glee (tea, to you and me). There was lots of talk about the Long Legs and the Little Long Legs. One thing they agreed on was that the Long Legs were not like the Tindims. It was still a complete mystery as to why they threw so much treasure away.

'I try to stop them,' said Tiddledim,
'but they insist it's rubbish. I have told
them the Tindims' motto, "Rubbish today
is treasure tomorrow," until I am blue in
the face.'

It was a puzzle to understand why the
Long Legs never seemed to listen.

Pinch wanted to ask Tiddledim a question, but so did everyone else. It was almost too much when Tiddledim told them he once had a purrtle, but that one day it had flown away.

Pinch held up his tail and his paw. 'Me, me,' he said. With his other paw on his little heart, he said, 'I found a purrtle egg and it hatched, and it grew.'

'Where is it?' said Tiddledim. 'Show me this wondrous sight.'

'The answer is,' said Pinch, 'as sad as a grey cloud in a blue sky. My purrtle flew away.'

Chapter Seven

Where Tiddledim tells them
about his purrtle and how
he came to find Rubbish
Island. He has a poem that
he shares with everyone.

'My purrtle did the same,' said Tiddledim. He stopped and thought for a moment. 'Of course, like me, you don't have a Bottlerama.'

'What's that got to do with my purrtle?' asked Pinch.

'Didn't you read my book with the chapter about looking after a purrtle?'

'No,' said Pinch.

'I called the chapter, The Ten Green Bottles,' said Tiddledim.

'Why didn't you call it, Looking after a Purrtle?' asked Pinch.

'My book is supposed to be read cover to cover,' said Tiddledim.

'Oh, I did that. I read each cover, I just didn't read the inside bit,' said Pinch.

Tiddledim sighed. 'A Bottlerama is an instrument made from ten green glass bottles. Each bottle is filled with different amounts of water and, when played, they make a sound as if the clouds are singing. A sound that comforts a purrtle.'

'Wow,' said Pinch. 'I think even I would come home if I heard the clouds singing.'

'But you are home,' said Brew.

It was then that Captain Spoons said, 'Haven't we been sitting here for a long time? The glee is drunk, the cakes are gone, the questions asked and answered, and yet the sun is still shining.'

'That is what I have been trying to tell you,' said Admiral Bonnet. 'Rubbish Island is too far north. We are now in the land where the sun doesn't set.'

'What, never?' asked Captain Spoons.

'No, not in the summer,' said Admiral Bonnet. 'But it goes to bed nearly all winter.'

'I should think the sun is exhausted,' said Captain Spoons. 'I mean, I would go to bed all winter if I had to stay up all summer.'

'Anyway,' said Admiral Bonnet, 'the reason we're here is that, once again, Bottle Hill is in the way. It's hard to see where I'm going.'

Tiddledim said, 'Well, I for one am glad you came this way. After all, I had hoped we would bump into one another and that you might have a working Bottlerama so I could sing my purrtle home. I put it in a poem. It is called The Right Way Wrong:

'I looked at this from upside down
And found the right way wrong.
I thought I had been a bit of a clown
There must be bottles for a song.

Another thought came to me
So I put my plan in motion.
That Rubbish Island has to be
Somewhere in this vast ocean.

I asked the walrus for his advice
You know he isn't hard to find.
He told me he had seen you twice
You'd been much on his mind.

So finally, I am here at last
Hoping to find a Bottlerama
Sweet music from the past
Ten bottles will end this little drama.'

63

'What, in the world of plastic cups, does that poem mean?' asked Brew.

'He is a writer,' whispered Skittle. 'Perhaps he has so many words inside him that he has to let them out somehow.'

'I think,' said Pinch, 'it is the most moving poem I have ever, and I mean ever, heard.'

'But what does it mean?' they said.

'It doesn't matter what it means. We need to find another five green bottles to make a Bottlerama,' said Pinch. 'And then my purrtle and Tiddledim's purrtle will come home. *And that's a fact actually.*'

Chapter Eight

Where Captain Spoons
makes pancakes and they
find that Tiddledim has
been hard at work that
neeptide.

Going to bed when the sun is still wide awake is a strange feeling.

Skittle, Pinch and Brew decided to sleep in the treehouse where the midnight sun kept an eye on them and the leaves rustled a lullaby.

Before he fell asleep, Pinch said, 'I hope, when I wake up, my purrtle is back. Green bottles or no green bottles.'

They woke to find the sun looking daisy-fresh. Captain Spoons was calling to say that pancakes were ready. It took them no time to jump out of bed.

Captain Spoons had put the table outside and they sat down to eat.

'Where's Tiddledim?' asked Pinch.

'Sleeping,' said Captain Spoons.

'I can't hear any snoring,' said Skittle.

'Perhaps he snores quietly,' said Brew.

'Don't be a daft toothbrush,' said Skittle. 'No Tindim does that.'

Spokes arrived as Captain Spoons was serving another plate of pancakes.

'I have been thinking about this Bottlerama,' said Spokes as he helped himself to a pancake.

'Yes,' said Pinch.

'And I think there must be at least one glass bottle in among the plastic ones on Bottle Hill.'

'All this talk of bottles makes me remember something,' said Captain Spoons. 'I dreamed that Bottle Hill had a massive hole in it, so we could see where we are going.'

'That is the best idea since recycled plastic rugs,' said Spokes. 'We might be able to do that.'

They set off to Bottle Hill. And there was Tiddledim already hard at work. He had found one small green glass bottle. But it wasn't that which made Captain Spoons say, 'Blow my tin hat into a trumpet.'

It was the massive round hole that Tiddledim had made, right in the middle of Bottle Hill.

'Good neeptide,' said Tiddledim. 'I woke early and thought I would have a rummage around to see if I could find any glass bottles. I am afraid to say I've only found one. Then another thought came to me about this hill. It needed a hole, big enough to see through. Now you will be able to steer the island where you want.'

'If that wasn't the same plan I'd dreamed up in my head,' said Captain Spoons, and he laughed.

'I hope you don't mind,' said Tiddledim.

'Mind? Never,' said Captain Spoons. 'The only thing that is bothering me is you haven't had any pancakes.'

'I have missed you, my friends,' said Tiddledim, laughing.

'And we have missed you,' said Admiral Bonnet.

And they laughed and laughed, right down to their toes until their tummies jelly-jiggled.

Chapter Nine

Where Tiddledim gets his
badge and Ethel comes
to tell them about a
whale in trouble.

That evening, the Tindims ate supper at Admiral Bonnet's house. Broom had brought a crate of Roo-Roo Pop. Today had been a special day. Never had so much been done in such a short space of time.

Pinch, Skittle and Brew had put on their Brightsea costumes. They always wore them for the Brightsea festival which happened once a year. All the Tindims would make fish costumes from the rubbish they had collected. Last time Brew had been a rainbow starfish, Skittle a glittering angel fish, and Pinch a pufferfish. He was sure that Tiddledim would like to see them. It was a jolly party.

Mug clapped her hands, and everyone
went quiet. 'I want to say a few words.'

'Hear, hear,' shouted Captain Spoons.

Mug said, 'If anyone deserves this
badge, it's you, Tiddledim.'

A loud cheer went up as she pinned the
badge on his jacket.

Tiddledim blushed blue and said, 'No, I
don't.'

'Well, we think you do,' said Mug.

Hitch Stitch stepped forward. 'Who

found the sixth green bottle for the Bottlerama?'

'Who helped me dig deep holes and plant more Roo-Roo trees?' said Broom.

'Who talked about all things purrtle with Pinch?' said Jug.

'Who made a hole in Bottle Hill?' said Spokes.

And they all said, 'The one and only Tiddledim the explorer, who talks to Little Long Legs and tells them about rubbish being treasure.'

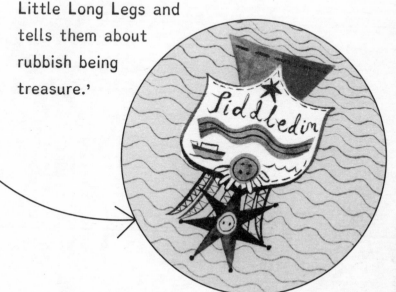

'Thank you very much,' said Tiddledim,
then stopped and looked about him.
'Where is Ethel B Dina?' he asked.

'My word,' said Admiral Bonnet.
'You're right. Why, in all the nautical
sunsets, isn't she here?'

'I will go and find her,' said Spokes.

Just then Ethel B Dina came running
towards them, quite out of breath. Her
lifesaver swan was a bit flat.

'My still and sparkling darlings,' she said. 'There is a whale lost at sea not far from Turtle Bay and heading towards the shore. I have had a message from the walrus, but it took me ages to understand what he was saying.'

'A whale?' said Captain Spoons, taking out his telescope. 'Where?'

'There,' shouted Brew. 'You can't miss it.'

'I see it,' said Broom.

'Oh no,' said Captain Spoons. 'I thought that was a large hill.'

'A hill with a water spout?' asked Broom.

'Dad,' said Skittle, 'you are looking through the telescope the wrong way.'

'Oh,' said Captain Spoons as he turned it around the right way. 'Wait a shingle shore, a whale? We must do something at once.'

'The walrus said that it's a young whale who has become separated from his mother. One of those Long Legs cruise ships passed by them, interrupting the mother whale while she was giving directions. So the young whale couldn't hear her and swam the wrong way. Now he isn't sure how to find her and his mother must be worried too,' said Ethel B Dina.

'This,' said Admiral Bonnet, 'is a rescue mission if ever I saw one.'

'That's a fact,' said Pinch.

Chapter Ten

Where Mug has a
brainwave. They row out
to the whale and Skittle
sings a lullaby.

'Wait, my still and sparkling darlings,' said Ethel B Dina. 'It is no good us all charging out there. He is a young and frightened whale. Tiddledim, can you row me and Hitch Stitch towards the dear creature?'

'I can,' said Tiddledim. 'I have the badge to prove it.'

'Good,' said Ethel. 'Oh, and we should take Skittle, as she knows a good whale

lullaby, just in case he swims off in the wrong direction.'

Captain Spoons thought it a fine and whale-saving idea. But he would be happier about it if Skittle stayed behind.

'Dad, please can I go?' said Skittle.

'What does your mum think?' asked Captain Spoons.

'I think you should sing your lullaby,' said Admiral Bonnet. 'How else are you going to become a brave-hearted Tindim, without an adventure or two?'

Granny Gull went to make up a picnic basket. 'A Tindim without food is a sad sight indeed,' she said.

Hitch Stitch collected coils of rope which she wrapped around herself. She said that there wasn't a situation, in her experience, where they didn't come in useful.

Broom added a few bottles of Roo-Roo Pop, in case they got thirsty. Jug gave them a blanket and Mug had a last-minute brainwave. She fetched the jumpers she had just finished knitting. Finally, they were off.

'It is a good thing,' said Ethel B Dina, 'that we are in the Land of the Midnight Sun. This would be much harder in the dark.'

The closer they came to the whale,
the easier it was to see the size of the
problem before them. It was ginormous.

'Now start singing, my still and
sparkling darling,' Ethel said to Skittle.

Skittle sang a lullaby, one that a

whale would understand. Ethel B Dina
climbed nimbly onto the giant creature's
back. Hitch Stitch made sure that the
rowing boat stayed alongside. She tied a
loose rope to the whale's tail and quickly
fastened it to the rowing boat.

There is an art to staying upright on a whale's back. Luckily, Ethel had mastered it. When she was close enough for the whale to hear, she called to Skittle to stop singing.

Ethel spoke gently to the whale and gave him directions as to which way to go. 'Don't worry, your mum is waiting for you,' she told him.

When she had finished, she asked the whale to stay still until she was back in the boat. But the minute she started to walk away the whale began to move.

'Skittle, sing!' shouted Ethel B Dina.

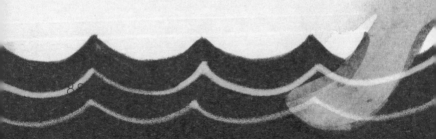

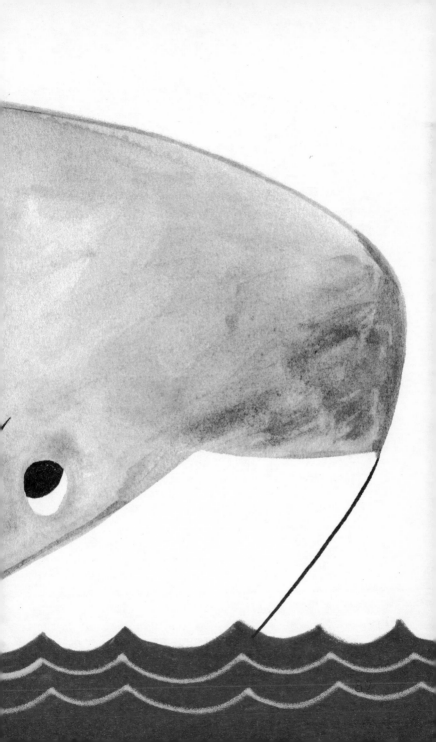

Skittle did her best. But now the whale could hear his mother calling and wanted to be home. He took off with a

WHOOSH

dragging the rowing boat with him.

Hitch Stitch, Skittle and Tiddledim all fell over. They lay at the bottom of the boat with their feet in the air as the rowing boat bounced along, pulled by the whale.

'What do we do now?' asked Skittle. 'And where is Ethel B Dina?'

Hitch Stitch managed to clamber up and as she did, the rope untangled from the whale. The rowing boat began to spin around and around. The whale flicked his tail and Ethel B Dina rose into the air, then landed back in the boat.

'I always land with a soft thought in my head,' she said. 'Soft, comfy thoughts cushion any fall.'

Skittle gave her a hug. 'Are you all right?'

'Yes, my still and sparkling darling, just a little on the soggy side. The main thing

is the whale knows which way to go. Now,
I think, like the whale, it is time for us to
go home too.'

Tiddledim pulled out his compass.
'Rubbish Island should be in that
direction,' he said.

They looked to where Rubbish Island used to be. Instead there was a lot of water. On the other side of them they could see land, and a shoreline with a shingle beach.

Where Rubbish Island used to be

Tiddledim's rowing boat

A shingle shore

95

'I think,' said Tiddledim, 'we should spend the night there.'

'You mean,' said Skittle, 'that we are not going home for supper and a bedtime story?'

'No,' said Tiddledim. 'Not tonight.'

Skittle had never been away from home, never left Rubbish Island, and never ever spent a night without Pinch. That was a lot of nevers for one day, she thought, and they made her feel a bit wobbly.

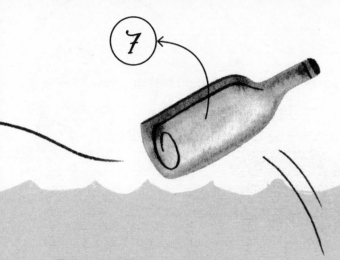

Ethel B Dina put an arm around her. 'Cheer up. You sang beautifully, my still and sparkling darling.'

They watched as the whale leaped out of the water with his mum, rolled over and dived again.

The whale flicked his tail and a perfect green glass bottle landed in the boat.

'That's how a whale says thank you,' said Ethel B Dina.

'Wow,' said Skittle. 'That makes seven glass bottles. All we need is three more.'

'That's the spirit,' said Tiddledim. 'You know what this is, Skittle?'

'No,' said Skittle.

'It is an adventure,' said Tiddledim. 'I'm rather fond of adventures and I am rather good at them too.'

Not far from the beach stood a large, painted red house.

'What is that?' asked Skittle.

'That is the house of a Long Leg,' said Tiddledim.

'They must be scary big.'

'Don't worry,' said Tiddledim. 'You won't be meeting them.'

They pulled the boat onto the shingle shore, near some rocks.

'This will do,' said Tiddledim, taking out the picnic basket and the Roo-Roo Pop.

'Thank goodness, my still and sparkling darlings, for Granny Gull,' said Ethel B Dina as they began to eat.

The evening was cool, and they were pleased that Mug had had her brainwave about jumpers and Jug had had his brainwave about a blanket.

Tiddledim was thinking that it might be a good idea to sleep in the rowing boat when they heard a sound, loud as thunder. They looked up to see a large pair of shoes.

Skittle said, 'Is that a Long Leg?'

'Yes,' said Tiddledim as the Long Leg picked up their rowing boat as if it were a toy.

Chapter Eleven

Where a Long Leg mistakes the Tindims' boat for a toy. And Hitch Stitch has to rescue the picnic basket.

'Leave it!' shouted Hitch Stitch bravely. 'That belongs to us, not you. Put it down this minute.'

'It's no good, he can't hear you,' said Tiddledim. 'After years and years of trying to talk to the Long Legs, the one thing I know is, you can't. It is something to do with growing up.'

The others stood well back as the Long Leg picked up the picnic basket and the bottles of Roo-Roo Pop. Hitch Stitch was not giving up. She grabbed hold of the Long Leg's trousers and the others watched as the Long Leg strode off towards the red house, with Hitch Stitch clinging on for dear life.

'Come on,' said Tiddledim. 'We have to get Hitch Stitch and our boat back.'

The red house looked huge to Skittle. The front door shut behind them with a bang.

They heard the Long Leg call out, 'I found this on the beach.'

Then another Long Leg asked, 'Did you see the whales out at sea?'

'Yes, there were two of them. A young calf and his mother.'

The two Long Legs talked about the whale and the rowing boat.

'A pity someone left such a lovely toy as this on the beach,' said the Long Leg.

'We didn't, and it isn't,' shouted Hitch Stitch, who had now let go of the Long Leg's trousers.

Ethel B Dina said, 'It's no good getting into a tizz, my still and sparkling darling. Best we listen rather than shout.'

'You're right,' said Hitch Stitch. 'It is just that we shouldn't be here.'

Tiddledim said that he was going to explore the house and that they should stay together until he came back. Skittle watched him go off through a forest of furniture and over fields of rugs.

Ethel B Dina listened carefully to what the Long Legs had to say. 'I think,' she said, 'a Little Long Leg is coming to stay tomorrow.'

'Watch out,' shouted Hitch Stitch as the chairs moved back and the Long Legs stood up and walked away.

Hitch Stitch didn't waste a moment. She threw her rope, the one with the hook on the end, up to the table. Then she climbed up it and rescued the picnic basket, carefully guiding it down to the floor.

Tiddledim returned to say that he had found a Little Long Leg's bedroom and it might be a good place to stay. Ethel B Dina took the picnic basket while Skittle and Hitch Stitch ran towards the open bedroom door.

It was a tidy room and, on a chair, there was a present with a ribbon tied around it.

Ethel B Dina told Tiddledim what she had heard.

'A Little Long Leg,' he said. 'Well, who would have thought we'd be so lucky? I'll be able to speak to them and then we can explain we need our boat back. Little Long Legs, unlike Long Legs, can see us and talk to us, which helps.'

Hitch Stitch used her rope to lasso the bed head. One by one, they climbed up onto the duvet, where there was a collection of toys.

Skittle felt tired. 'Is this what you call an adventure?' she asked sleepily.

'Yes, I think so,' said Hitch Stitch. 'In fact, I know so.'

'Then, maybe, I would rather not be having one,' said Skittle. 'I think adventures could be fun, if you can get home in time for tea.'

Ethel put an arm around her. 'I quite agree,' she said. 'You could curl up with that bear and I will take the rabbit. Hitch Stitch can have the sheep.'

Tiddledim said that he would stay awake and keep guard.

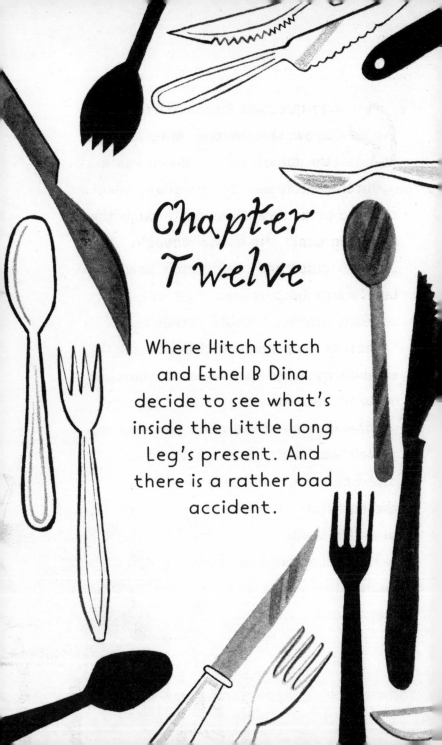

Chapter Twelve

Where Hitch Stitch and Ethel B Dina decide to see what's inside the Little Long Leg's present. And there is a rather bad accident.

'**G**ood neeptide,' said Skittle the following morning. 'What are you two doing?'

Hitch Stitch was on the chair, checking out the present by peeping through the wrapping paper. 'It is as I thought,' she said. 'A glass bottle. I think it's green, but I can't be sure until the wrapping paper is off.'

'Let me help you,' said Ethel, as she climbed from the bed down to the chair.

'Wait,' said Skittle. 'You can't just go opening someone else's present.'

Neither Ethel nor Hitch Stitch could hear her over the noise of the wrapping paper being undone.

'Oh,' said Ethel. 'There's something else with it.'

'There's a plastic pot too,' said Hitch Stitch. 'You take the top off the bottle, and I'll take the top off the pot so we can see what's inside.'

'Where is Tiddledim?' asked Skittle, who felt sure that neither Ethel B Dina nor Hitch Stitch should be doing what they were doing.

Ethel pulled the top off the bottle and Hitch Stitch managed to remove the top from the plastic pot. Hitch Stitch dipped her hand into the pot and slime spilled onto the chair. It was very slippery.

Ethel B Dina skidded off the chair, knocking the bottle over as she fell. Down went the plastic pot. Hitch Stitch tried to help but she went slip-sliding too, crashing down after the pot.

Skittle couldn't bear to look. 'Is anything broken?' she asked.

Hitch Stitch said, 'Well, the chair is still standing. The good news is the bottle isn't broken. But the bad news is, I think we are in big trouble.'

'Why?' asked Skittle.

'I don't think Ethel B Dina landed with a soft thought in her head,' replied Hitch Stitch.

Chapter Thirteen

Where Ethel B Dina ends up in a lot of trouble and Tiddledim has to give her some of his rescue potion.

hatever was in the plastic pot was seeping onto the floor, where Ethel B Dina was lying flat out, her lifesaver ring very deflated.

'Ethel,' said Hitch Stitch. 'Talk to me.'

Skittle climbed off the bed and went to help. By now there was a lot of cold, damp, sticky gunk coming out of the pot.

'Help me get Ethel up,' said Hitch Stitch.

She and Skittle tried to move, but the more they tried, the more stuck they became, as Ethel lay there like a flattened starfish.

What are we going to do?

At that moment Tiddledim rushed back to tell them that the Long Legs had gone out in the car, and he'd found their rowing boat. If they were quick, they could make their escape.

Before Skittle could warn him, Tiddledim had skidded in the green gooey mess and done a flying somersault.

'What's happened?' he said when he saw Ethel B Dina.

'She fell off the chair,' said Skittle. 'And so did Hitch Stitch. Then the bottle and pot landed on top of Ethel. It is lucky the bottle didn't break.' With much difficulty, Tiddledim the explorer made it through the slime to Ethel B Dina's side.

'Don't worry, my dear lady of the still and sparkling delights, we will have you back on your tippy tippy-toes.' He took out a flask that he kept in his jacket pocket for just such an emergency. 'It is rescue potion,' he said. 'It works on most things,' and he gave Ethel two spoonfuls.

'Now what?' said Skittle when nothing happened. 'Let's try and sit her up.'

But the more they moved, the more stuck they became.

'Oh, bosh, tosh,' said Tiddledim. 'Perhaps a third spoon might do the trick.'

Only after another spoonful did Ethel open one eye and then the other.

'Oh, my still and sparkling darlings, are we home yet?' she asked.

'No,' said Tiddledim. 'How are you feeling?'

'A little deflated,' said Ethel.

'What's that sound?' asked Skittle.

'The Long Legs are coming back,' said Tiddledim. 'Usually, at this point, I run and hide. Then I explain who I am. But we can't leave Ethel here. Anyway, we are stuck in this slime. We'll have to be brave.'

They waited. Skittle held her breath
as the bedroom door opened. At first,
the Little Long Leg didn't see them, as
she was half-in the room and half-out,
talking to the Long Legs.

'She might scream,' Tiddledim
whispered. 'I have known it to happen.
Be prepared.'

'I will, Granny,' said the Little Long
Leg. 'I'll unpack my things first.' She
dropped her bag and then stopped and
stared.

'Are you all right, Anna?' the Long Legs called.

'Yes,' said the Little Long Leg.

'Have you seen the slime? It's a present for you. And I put some glitter in the bottle for you to play with.'

'It's the best. Thank you, Granny,' she said and closed the door.

Tiddledim managed to stand upright. He said, 'We are the Tindims of Rubbish Island and we are slime-bound.'

Chapter Fourteen

Where the Little
Long Leg saves the day
and has a great idea
about how more Little
Long Legs could get to
know about the Tindims.

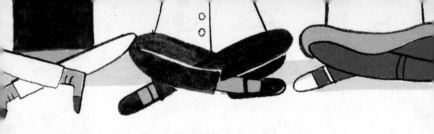

'Wow,' said the Little Long Leg. 'Tindims. I've heard of you.'

'You have?' said Tiddledim.

'Yes, you went to my best friend's school and talked about rubbish. None of the teachers could see you, but my best friend thought you were well wicked.'

'Would you be so kind as to help us?' asked Tiddledim.

Anna lifted Ethel B Dina out of the slime first and put her on the bed to rest.

Skittle pulled slime off her face. 'We helped a baby whale get back to his mum, and then the Long Legs took away our rowing boat. This neeptide we opened your present because we wanted to know if if there was a green glass bottle inside.'

'It's my fault,' said Hitch Stitch, and she explained what had happened.

'What is your name?' asked Anna.

'My name is Hitch Stitch,' said Hitch Stitch.

Anna put her on the bed so that she could sit next to Ethel B Dina.

'I am Skittle,' said Skittle. 'And we want to go home to Rubbish Island.'

Anna set to work cleaning up the slime. 'We do need to get back to Rubbish Island,' said Tiddledim. 'But your grandfather has our boat.'

'I will tell him to give it back,' said Anna.' You can keep the bottle too.'

'Thank you, but the Long Legs can't see us. Only you can,' said Tiddledim.

'Wait,' said Anna 'I have an idea.' She took out a sketchbook. 'Will you let me draw you? And maybe I could write down some of the things you say. Afterwards, I promise I will get the boat back.'

'This isn't going to take too long, is it?' asked Skittle.

'No, not long,' said Anna. She drew them with their jumpers on because they were all a bit chilly after the slime.

'This is amazing. Wow. Can you talk about yourselves?'

'Why?' asked Skittle.

'I am going to do my summer project for school on the Tindims of Rubbish Island.'

Hitch Stitch said, 'The thing is we still need two more green glass bottles.'

'That's easy,' said Anna. 'I can get two more for you from the recycling bin.'

'Wow,' said Skittle. 'We're always saying, "Long Legs, please don't throw rubbish in the sea." Perhaps it's working. Your granny and grandpa are recycling. If more Long Legs know about us, even if they can't see us, maybe they will do the same with the Little Long Legs to help them.'

Anna wrote it all down. Tiddledim told her about his purrtle and the Bottlerama. Hitch Stitch showed her how to tie one of her knots, which Anna tried to draw, but said it was actually a bit too hard.

'Can we go home now?' asked Skittle.

'Wait,' said Ethel B Dina as she was being helped down off the bed. 'Don't forget we need two more green bottles.'

'I won't,' said Anna. 'But will they fit in your little rowing boat?'

'I have rope,' said Hitch Stitch. 'We can tow them behind us.'

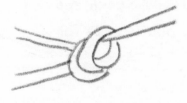

As they walked down to the beach, with Anna holding the little rowing boat and oars, Skittle explained to her why they needed the three green bottles.

'Will you be able to get back to Rubbish Island?' Anna asked when their boat was bobbing in the water. All four bottles (including the Whale's bottle) had been tied together by Hitch Stitch and attached to the rowing boat, ready for their journey.

'Yes,' said Tiddledim. He took out his compass. 'I know the way.'

'I nearly forgot your picnic basket,' said Anna. She took it from her pocket.

Just then they heard the Long Legs calling that lunch was ready. Anna turned to look at the house and shout, 'I'm coming.'

When she turned again, the Tindims had already set off. She could see them in the distance, waving goodbye.

Chapter Fifteen

Where the Tindims are very worried indeed about what has happened to Skittle, Hitch Stitch, Tiddledim and Ethel B Dina. And Granny Gull bakes a cake.

Admiral Bonnet and Captain Spoons were as worried as any Tindim could be about Skittle. Not to mention Ethel B Dina, Hitch Stitch and Tiddledim. What had happened to them? It was a question the Tindims wanted answered.

Captain Spoons imagined the worst, that the rowing boat had sunk. Pinch said that if that had happened, he would know about it.

'How?' asked Captain Spoons.

And for the first time, Pinch didn't feel like saying, '*That's a fact.*' For the fact was, the thought of losing Skittle was far worse than losing a purrtle. It would be the end of everything in his world.

Brew, who wasn't given to drama usually, agreed. 'I mean,' he said, 'we are now the only Tindims left. And there weren't that many of us to start with.'

Pinch cried, 'I want my Skittle back. After all, I am her furry, purry, one and only pet and I fret a lot about her. And *that is a fact actually*!' he wailed.

Spokes thought it was best to be doing something other than moping.

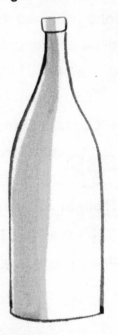

He started to make a Bottlerama. He was
sure he could make it sound good with six
bottles, for six is better than none.

Granny Gull knew the only thing to do, when nothing could be done, was to bake. She decided to bake Skittle's favourite cake. At teatime, she put out tables and chairs and hung up paper lanterns.

'But won't this make it a hundred times worse,' asked Barnacle Bow, 'and one thousand times sadder, if they don't come back today?'

'The smell of a newly baked cake is always tempting,' said Granny Gull.

The only Tindim who was cheerful was Baby Cup. Mug had taken her with her

to ask Admiral
Bonnet if there was
any news. Baby Cup, who
was looking out to sea, called,
'Skittle.'

Broom was standing on the top
branch of a Roo-Roo tree and
didn't see Skittle. Neither did
Admiral Bonnet.

But Spokes did and
excitedly he shouted,

'Boat ahoy, boat ahoy.'

There was Skittle at the helm, waving her jumper as if it were a flag, and Tiddledim rowing like mad. Broom made it to the beach, waded to the boat and started to pull it ashore.

139

Captain Spoons did a jig and shed a
tear when he saw Skittle. Pinch rushed
here and there and nowhere, except into
Skittle's arms. And everyone hugged
everyone else.

'Now,' said Broom, 'we have ten green
bottles, and that means...'

'We have a
proper Bottlerama,'
said Spokes.

Chapter Sixteen

Where, after an adventure, there is a party and a sing-song. And everything on Rubbish Island is well and good.

Next day, after a sound night's sleep, even though the sun hadn't yet gone to bed, Rubbish Island had found the slip tide. Tiddledim's boat was pulled along with the island, towards warmer water.

In the ebbtide, Spokes brought out a brand new Bottlerama. Everyone agreed he had made a fine instrument.

'When you are ready,' said Spokes to Ethel B Dina. She had been thinking for a long time about a song. She cleared her throat.

'On the sea and a worried whale
Made the brave Tindims set sail.
With a roll of the oar,
they rowed away
Let's rescue that whale,
they did say.

And, ho, ho, my darlings
We helped a whale home.
We helped a whale home.

An adventure is lovely,
But no more will we roam.
No more will we roam.

Now the whale is home, home, home.'

Oh, the sea and a worried whale ♪♪♪♪♪♪♪♪

It was a jolly song that rose and fell in all the right places and had a chorus. It sounded like the clouds were singing too. In fact, the Tindims weren't quite sure if it was they who were singing, or if the clouds were joining in.

Everyone sang together, and they were so carried away that they almost forgot why they needed a Bottlerama in the first place.

Made the brave Tindims set sail.

Above them were
not one, not two
and hardly three.
But more than four and
all very much of five.
Most definitely six, not
to mention seven. But then
again, it could be eight and
was most probably nine.
And finally, there was
no mistaking, ten. Ten
purrtles had landed
on Rubbish Island.
And that, said
Pinch, *is a fact.*

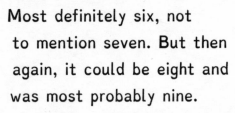
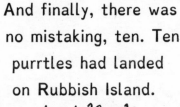

The TINDIMS
of Rubbish Island

Meet Skittle, her furry purry
pet, Pinch, and her best friend
Brew as they set off on their first
adventure on Rubbish Island.

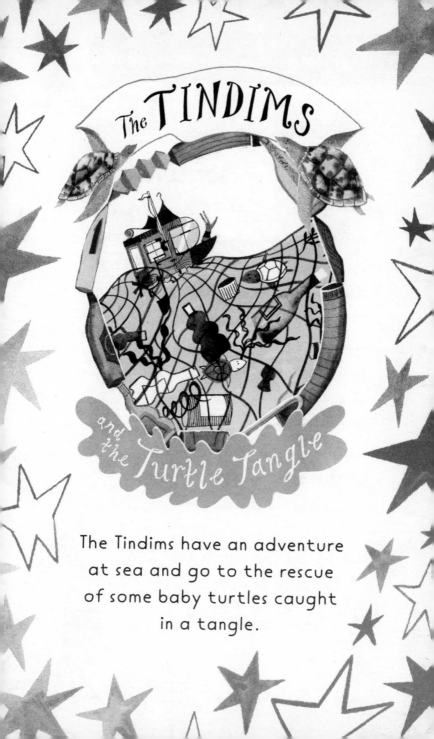

The TINDIMS

and the Turtle Tangle

The Tindims have an adventure
at sea and go to the rescue
of some baby turtles caught
in a tangle.

Did you spot me while you were reading?

'Rubbish today is treasure tomorrow.'

BOTTLE TOP FUN

Make a snake by collecting as many bottle tops as you can, then with the help of a Long Leg, thread them on a string and paint.

Make bottle top creatures by sticking your bottle tops to card or a lollipop stick. Paint them, give them eyes and decorate them any way you like – see how many different creatures you can make.

Help keep beaches clean!
Tell the Long Legs to pick up litter and take it home!